JANE KURTZ AND CHRISTOPHER KURTZ

Water Hole Waiting

PICTURES BY
LEE CHRISTIANSEN

Greenwillow Books
An Imprint of HarperCollinsPublishers

Morning slinks onto the savanna
and licks up the night shadows
one by one. Crickets stop chirping.
A frog plops softly into the water hole.

The silence pokes Monkey's ear.
He opens his eyes with a thirsty
grunt and bounces down the tree.
Time to jump. Time to swing.
Time for morning foraging.

Sun cartwheels
slowly up the sky,
herding
hippopotami.
The grasslands
fill with birdcalls,
wails, a loud
buzz-buzzing
of insects,
a great
swish-swishing
of tails.

Monkey thinks it's time for a drink.

Wait! Mama grabs his paw.

Stay away from Hippo's yawning jaws.

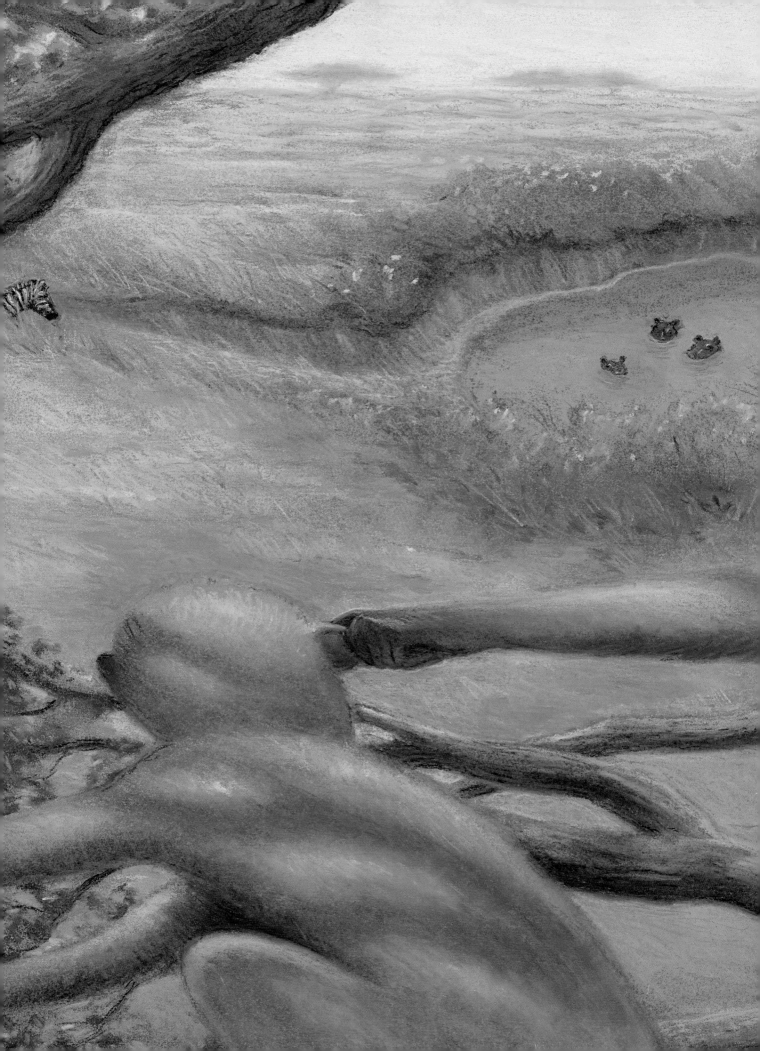

Sun climbs the sky
like an acrobat and
dangles at the top.
Heat sizzles the savanna,
heavy on monkey fur.

Monkey stares
at the water hole.
The hippo trail
appears to be clear.
Wait!
Mama grabs his ear.

Swish, swush. Snort and grunt.

The grazers are coming down the path.

Look out for sharp hooves and quick kicks.

Splish, splush. Zebra wades near
the lumpy log with hooded eyes.
Slurp, slush. Wet and cool.
Slash, snap! White splash and
bone jaw burst from the pool.
Zebra is one moment quicker than death.
The log sinks back and waits.

Sun bristles, bright and round.

Monkey's feet nibble the ground.

Prance, dance, take a little chance.

His feet find their way to the hippo trail.

Wait! Mama grabs his tail.

Slip, slap. Lion is padding down the path, not looking right, not looking left. Beware of Lion, who crouches close and lip-laps water between razor teeth.

Mama closes tired eyes.
Monkey nips a few steps closer,
skips and slips a little bit closer.
Rumble, rumble.
What's that sound?
A grumble like thunder
thumps the ground.
Wait! Mama grabs his leg.
Whoa. Slow. No, no, no.
Back to the trees
to munch on seeds.

Thrum, thrum. Elephant comes rumbling down the path. Gentle shuffling. Tender trunk. Elephant has eyes only for family. Steer clear of heavy feet and reckless splashing.

Sun somersaults
down the sky.
Monkey's throat
is parched
and aching.
Monkey's fur
is almost baking.
Monkey's toes
are ready to go.
Wait!
Mama grabs
his neck.

Gulup, galumpf. Giraffe is swaying down the path. Time mooooves slo...o...owly around Giraffe. Neck bends, legs splay. Will lips ever go so low that they touch cool water?

Evening slinks across the savanna, pulling shadows behind it. The grasses start to whisper. Sun lands on the horizon and tucks away its lower half. Nobody, nobody is moving on the path. Floating in water, the log watches. Crocodile waits for one
careless
step.

Monkey's thirsty throat is burning. He starts bouncing, squeaking, squirming.
Hurry scurry up!
Monkeys scamper down the trail. Quick, no laggers.
No lollygaggers.

Eek! Take care. Beware, beware.

Monkeys tumble back.

SNAP!

Evening sighs. Sun sinks.
Crocodile ripples away.

As crickets start chirping,
a frog strikes a drumbeat—
cha-chug-chug,
cha-chug-chug-chug.
In the still-warm air,
the monkeys leap
jiggle
chitter-chatter
wiggle
all the way down
to the waiting water hole.
Aaaaah.

AUTHORS' NOTE

Although this story is fiction, it is possible to learn many things about life on the African savanna from it. Anyone who has sat and watched a water hole for a while (something you may try via cyberspace by visiting www.AfriCam.com) notices that the animals seem to take turns. Elephants wander up. Buffalo wander off. And so on. During the hot dry season when there is less moisture in the grasses and other savanna vegetation, water holes are busier. Sometimes, especially during this dry time, different species will drink at a water hole together.

The main characters in our story are vervet monkeys. The mothers spend a lot of time near their young ones. Vervets have special calls to signal danger from predators. When most vervets hear the leopard alarm, they run for the trees; when they hear the eagle alarm, they look up; and when they hear the snake alarm, they stand on their back legs and look around in the grass. They have a less urgent alarm call for animals that could be dangerous but do not hunt them regularly, such as hyenas and lions. They even have a warning call for unfamiliar humans.

The water hole in *Water Hole Waiting* has steep sides and a narrow hippo trail leading down to it, so the monkeys wait even when animals that do not prey on monkeys, such as elephants, are drinking. A monkey wouldn't want to share close quarters with a large animal that could accidentally hurt it. Since most water holes have some spot where a monkey could scramble down and drink away from such large animals, most monkeys don't have to wait until evening for a drink. Still, whether you're a thirsty monkey hanging back while a lion drinks or a person hiding near a water hole hoping to spot a parade of animals, waiting is never easy.

For Mom and Dad, who made travels on the East African savanna a great adventure—J. K.

For Erin, who has Africa in her veins, Hannah, who somersaults across the sky,
and Jacob, who can hardly wait—C. K.

For Lori, the patient one—L. C.

We thank Dr. Lynne A. Isbell of the University of California at Davis for her kind assistance.—J. K., C. K., and L. C.

Library of Congress Cataloging-in-Publication Data: Kurtz, Jane. Water hole waiting / by Jane Kurtz and Christopher Kurtz; illustrated by Lee Christiansen.   p.   cm. "Greenwillow Books." Summary: A thirsty monkey waits as the larger animals drink from the water hole on the African savanna. ISBN 0-06-029850-2 (trade). ISBN 0-06-029851-0 (lib. bdg.). 1. Cercopithecus aethiops—Juvenile fiction. [1. Vervet monkey—Fiction. 2. Monkeys—Fiction. 3. Zoology—Africa—Fiction. 4. Animals—Fiction.] I. Kurtz, Christopher. II. Christiansen, Lee, ill. III. Title.   PZ10.3.K9735 Wat 2002 [E]—dc21 2001023040. 10 9 8 7 6 5 4 3   First Edition